3 1994 00915 3534

NOV 1 6 1998

AUG   1 2007

SANTA ANA PUBLIC LIBRARY

D0518033

WASHING the WILLOW TREE LOON

BY JACQUELINE BRIGGS MARTIN
ILLUSTRATED BY NANCY CARPENTER

J PICT BK MARTIN, J.
Martin, Jacqueline
Washing the willow tree
loon
$16.00
CENTRAL   31994009153534

SIMON & SCHUSTER BOOKS FOR YOUNG READERS

ACKNOWLEDGMENT

I would like to thank the people at Tri-State Bird Rescue and Research in Newark, Delaware, for generously sharing information learned from their hundreds of hours of bird washing and bird care. They have answered many questions and given me much helpful advice regarding the story. Should there be errors, they are my errors, not the errors of those who took time from their work to talk to me or read this story.

    A portion of the proceeds from the sale of this book will be donated to Tri-State Bird Rescue and Research.   —J.B.M.

SIMON & SCHUSTER BOOKS FOR YOUNG READERS
An imprint of Simon & Schuster Children's Publishing Division
1230 Avenue of the Americas, New York, NY 10020
Text copyright © 1995 by Jacqueline Briggs Martin
Illustrations copyright © 1995 by Nancy Carpenter
All rights reserved, including the right of reproduction in whole or in part in any form.
SIMON & SCHUSTER BOOKS FOR YOUNG READERS is a trademark of Simon & Schuster.
Designed by Christy Hale
The text of this book is set in Flareserif Light.
The illustrations were rendered in oil paint and color pencil on paper.
Manufactured in Hong Kong by South China Printing Company (1988) Ltd.
10 9 8 7 6 5 4 3 2 1
Library of Congress Cataloging-in-Publication Data
Martin, Jacqueline Briggs.
Washing the willow tree loon / by Jacqueline Briggs Martin ; illustrated by Nancy Carpenter.—1st ed.
p.   cm.
Summary: A loon is rescued from an oil spill, cleaned, and cared for before being returned to the wild.
Includes information on cleaning birds.
ISBN 0-689-80415-6
1. Loons—Juvenile fiction.   [1. Oil spills—Fiction.   2. Loons—Fiction. 3. Wildlife rescue—Fiction.]
I. Carpenter, Nancy, ill.   II. Title.
PZ10.3.M4425Bi 1995
[E]—dc20   94-11787

For those who stop to watch herons or listen to loons—
and all who love and care for swimmers and flyers
—J. B. M.

For Kevin
—N. C.

ONE FALL NIGHT a barge hit a bridge and
spilled a rushing stream of oil into Turtle Bay.
Many diving birds—the loons and diving ducks—
dived into the oily stream and were covered with oil.
Many swimming and floating birds
swam through the oily stream and were covered with oil.

The loon that stayed by the fallen willow tree
was covered with oil. Her feathers,
which had kept out water better than any raincoat,
were matted and sticky and too heavy to help her fly.
She shivered, swam to the shallows by the bend in the road,
and began to use her bill to clean her feathers.

In the morning the first person who saw the loon drove on past. "What's one bird? It's not my worry," she said. "The world is full of birds, and I have work to do."

In the afternoon a housepainter with a long-handled net came to net the bird. His grandfather had taught him how to be quiet around birds.
Others had shown him how to catch oiled birds.
But the loon was frightened and dived into the water— out of reach of the long-handled net.

The painter picked up another bird,
one that had died from the oil.
He put the bird into a bag, so it could be studied,
and so no other animal would eat the bird
and get sick from the oil.
   The housepainter waited to see the loon again
but did not find her.
He walked on to look for other birds.
"This place has many birds," he said.
"And I have work to do."
   In the evening the loon went back to the shallows
by the bend in the road and slept.

In the early morning a woman in tall fishing boots
walked through the shallow water. Quietly, quietly,
she came to the loon and netted her. She owned a bakeshop
but made no cakes when there were birds to be cleaned.
"Bird work is thanks for the songs I hear
when I am baking in the early morning," she said.
  The baker and a friend took the bird out of the net,
gently wrapped a towel around her body, and
carried the loon to empty boxes on a waiting truck.

The baker checked to be sure the box had air holes.
She put a soft cloth on the bottom of the box
for the loon to rest on, then placed the loon
inside the box, inside the warm truck.

"The day is full of shivering birds," she said.
"And I have work to do."

The truck took the willow tree loon and
the other rescued birds—the ducks, the geese,
and the herons—to an old school building
where there were trained workers to help them.

A barber with gentle hands used a cotton swab
to wipe the oil from the loon's mouth and breathing holes.
Carefully he washed the loon's eyes with clean, warm water.

He said, "I will see the world in birds' eyes today.
I have work to do." And he went to pick up another bird.

An animal doctor felt the loon for broken bones
and fed her water and medicine through a tube
into her stomach. The medicine would help the loon
get over the oil she had taken in while cleaning her wings.
The doctor had tried to mend broken robins' wings
when she was young. But the robins had always died.
Now she knew what to do. She put the bird in a quiet pen
to rest from the scare of many hands and strange sounds.
"This place is noisy with people who all have work to do,"
said the doctor.

Late that night a young man came to the schoolhouse
and took the loon from the pen where she was resting.
He once had a pet duck named Ralph. He called
all the birds Ralph, and he whispered songs to them
while he poured warm, soapy water over their feathers.

Two others helped him hold the loon in the washtub
and keep her calm. He rubbed her feathers gently
to clean away the oil. When the water was dirty with oil
they moved the loon to another tub full of fresh water.
The young man used cloth and swabs to clean away the oil.
"Three tubs of water to clean this bird," he said.
"I have work to do."

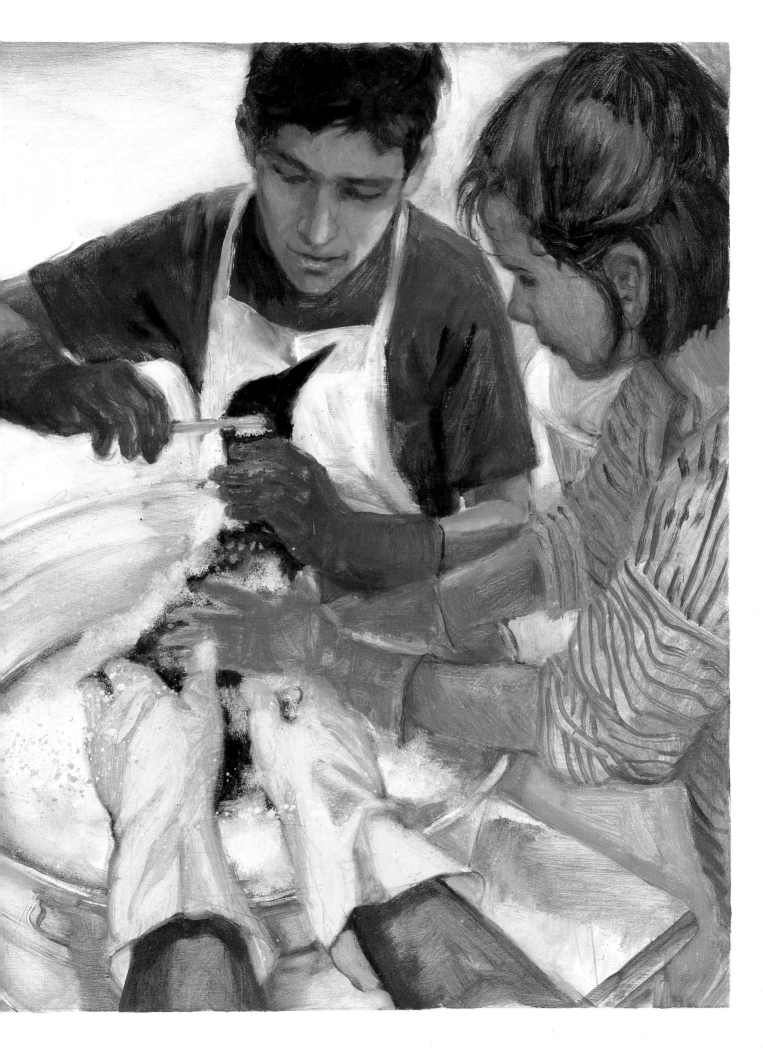

At the rinsing tub
was an old woman who
still kept the empty shell of
a hummingbird egg she had found
fifty years ago. "It's no bigger than a bean,"
she said. "But it started me out with birds."
She had a lifetime of bird stories. Neighbors who
wanted to see hummingbirds came to her house.

She rinsed the loon four times, gently spraying with
clean, warm water to wash away the soap. She sprayed until
plump drops of water looked like beads on the bird's back. Two
others helped her hold the bird and keep her calm. Then they dried
the loon with towels and put her in a pen with pillows and heat lamps.
"This is your world for now. And you have work to do," the woman
said. The loon began to preen her feathers.

Later, the old woman carried the bird to a
deep pool, where she could swim, dive, eat, and preen.
The old woman came back many times and watched
until the willow tree loon was swimming easily
and her feathers were as good as a new raincoat.

An artist who painted pictures of birds
came in the early morning. He left his easel
and his paints when it was time to set the birds free.
He placed a towel over the loon and put her in a box.
    He drove to a place where the water was clean.
He knew that the loon could not walk on the shore.
So he waded out until the water reached his knees,
opened the box, and gently tipped it.
He watched as the loon righted herself and swam away.

That night, the baker, the young man,
the barber, the housepainter, the doctor,
the woman who loved hummingbirds,
the artist, and all the helpers
listened for the loon.

Who knows who has heard or seen
the willow tree loon since then.
Maybe me, maybe you.
The world is full of birds.
And we have work to do.

A NOTE ABOUT BIRD REHABILITATION

Oil spills large enough to damage birds happen thousands of times each year in the inland and coastal waters of the United States.

Oil can be harmful to birds in many ways. A bird's feathers trap air. That trapped air helps keep the bird warm, helps it to float and to fly. Oiled feathers cannot trap air. The oil that a bird swallows as it cleans its feathers can damage kidneys, intestines, lungs, or the liver. Then the bird cannot digest food or water. Birds that have taken in oil can have trouble laying eggs that will hatch into healthy young.

The oil from one oiled feather can kill the eggs of a roosting bird. Oil can also injure the stomach and other organs of animals that eat oiled birds.

Water birds—even injured water birds—are wary of humans and may use their last bit of energy to avoid being caught. Volunteers who catch and treat birds have had many hours of training to learn just what to do. They must have a permit from the federal government allowing them to rehabilitate native birds. Those who supervise the volunteers must have special health and safety training so that neither they nor any of the other volunteers will be harmed by the spilled oil.

The volunteers know they will have their best success if they go out in the early morning and move quietly but steadily from the water to the shore toward the oiled birds. Birds are less frightened when they cannot see. Covering a bird with a towel calms it and makes it easier for the worker to carry the bird without hurting it or being hurt by the bird.

The willow tree loon was taken to an old school building. A treatment center could be set up in any building with lots of water and good space for pens. Some pens are built from plywood. But sometimes children's playpens are used for the birds. Some water birds—loons and grebes—have a hard time keeping their balance when they are not swimming. They must have soft bedding in their pens—air mattresses, crumpled newspapers, water pillows, or bubble packing material—so that they do not injure their chests. Towels and other washable cloths serve as the top layer of bedding. This must be changed at least twice a day.

Oiled birds are given special water and medicine through tubes into their stomachs. If the birds are too weak to hold up their heads, the medicine and water is put directly into their veins. It may be hours or even days before the birds are strong enough to stand being cleaned.

Feathers must be cleaned very gently. People who wash birds have been carefully trained. It is not a job we can do

at the kitchen sink. Washing and rinsing one bird takes about an hour and uses about 150 gallons of water. That much water would fill four bathtubs. Rinsing is very important. If any soapy water remains on a bird's feathers, they will not be waterproof.

Just like the loon in this story, cleaned birds are placed in a drying pen, where they can preen their feathers. Preening feathers puts them back in the right place. It is more important than combing hair is for people. Without the right placement, feathers will not be able to trap the small pockets of air that keep the bird from being too hot or too cold and help it to float and to fly. Without the right placement of feathers, the bird will not be waterproof.

As with our willow tree loon, cleaned and dried birds are finally placed in pools, where they can swim. Sometimes water birds in captivity don't want to eat. Swimming seems to make the birds more interested in eating. Swimming also causes birds to do more preening and so helps them become waterproof. Right after cleaning, birds will only be able to swim for a short time before their feathers absorb water and they begin to sink. Then they must be removed from the pool and placed under heat lamps. Gradually, birds preen their feathers into the right arrangement, and they are able to swim for longer periods of time. Loons should be able to remain in water

for a day and still have dry feathers before they are released.

Other signs that a bird is ready to go back into the wild are that it has a normal body temperature, preens, and tries to defend itself against handlers.

Most of the oiled birds that are brought to a well-run treatment center can be successfully treated and released back into the wild. But many oiled birds escape the nets and are never brought in.

Oil is a danger to water birds. But there are dangers to other kinds of birds, too. Some are shot. Some are wounded by cats or hit by cars. Some are poisoned or caught in traps. These birds can be helped at a licensed bird rehabilitation clinic, where animal doctors and volunteers who know just what to do work together.

To find out if there is a bird rehabilitation clinic in your area, check with the U.S. Fish and Wildlife Service, your local chapter of the Society for the Prevention of Cruelty to Animals, or a local veterinarian.

Cleaning oiled birds is one way of helping wildlife. But there are many other ways. Our work could be figuring out how to use less oil in our lives. It could be volunteering to help clean up a junk-filled stream to make a better place for fish and water birds. It could be planting some shrubs or trees that will provide winter food—seeds or berries—for birds. The world is losing birds, and we have work to do.